MIGHTY MORPHIN
POWER
RANGERS™
1

THE ULTIMATE

TEAM

The Power Rangers™ are here to fight Rita Repulsa™ and her forces of evil. Each one of the Power Rangers has a different skill and personality that makes them special. The members, students of Angel Grove High, all work together to make the ultimate team.

The Red Ranger is the leader of the team. He draws his power from the Tyrannosaurus Rex. His weapon is the Power Sword and his vehicle is the Tyrannosaurus Dinozord™. He also pilots the Megazord™.

RED RANGER

Able to crush a rock into pieces, the Red Ranger's kick is a powerful force. His jump-kick is even more powerful!

JASON ● RED RANGER

Jason is a seventeen year old black belt in karate and is also the Red Ranger. He is serious about his martial arts and spends much of his time working out new moves and perfecting old ones.

Tyrannosaurus Dinozord™

Piloted by the Red Ranger, the Tyrannosaurus Dinozord uses its claws to attack enemies. The powerful tail can also act as a whip to defeat opponents.

POWER GUN™

POWER SWORD™

Mastodon Dinozord™

Piloted by the Black Ranger, the Mastodon Dinozord is very big and heavy. It is capable of freezing enemies by shooting a cold blast of air through its snout.

Black Ranger's skills show as he defeats his opponent. Black Ranger is in full force!

ZACK●BLACK RANGER

Zack is everybody's friend and lights up a room when he enters it. He is smooth talking, street-wise and very clever and has the ability to disarm his adversaries with a quick smile and a smooth line.

POWER AXE™

BLACK RANGER™

Zack is the Black Ranger. He draws his power from the mighty Mastodon. His weapon is the Power Axe and he drives the Mastodon Dinozord.

YELLOW RANGER™

Trini is the Yellow Ranger. The Yellow Ranger is among the quickest of the group. Her powers come from the vicious Sabertooth Tiger. Her weapon is the Power Dagger™ and she drives the Sabertooth Tiger Dinozord.

POWER DAGGER™

TRINI●YELLOW RANGER

Trini is usually quiet but quite intelligent. She is very patient but only to a certain point. If pushed over the limit, she becomes a razor-sharp fighter with lightning reflexes. She is very active in school events.

Sabertooth Tiger Dinozord™

The Sabertooth Tiger Dinozord is very fast. It can speed across the ground and outrun any enemy. Its tail can act as a cannon to help defeat Rita's monsters.

The Yellow Ranger's kick is more than meets the eye. Her quickness makes the kicks lethal.

The Pink Ranger is able to defeat strong enemies in a flash.

KIMBERLY
●PINK RANGER

Kimberly is a lively and beautiful girl who loves shopping and gymnastics. She is a city champion gymnast and she brings this skill with her into her life as a Power Ranger.

POWER BOW™

Pterodactyl Dinozord™

The only Dinozord™ that can fly, the Pterodactyl Dinozord uses radar to check out the enemies. It also has a beam cannon to defend itself against enemies.

PINK RANGER™

Kimberly is the Pink Ranger. The Pink Ranger is very acrobatic due to Kimberly's gymnastics background. She draws power from the amazing Pterodactyl. Her weapon is the Power Bow and her vehicle is the Pterodactyl Dinozord.

BLUE RANGER™

Billy is the Blue Ranger. The Blue Ranger thinks before he makes his moves. His power comes from the Triceratops. His weapon is the Power Lance and his vehicle is the Triceratops Dinozord™.

BILLY●BLUE RANGER

Billy is an ultra-intelligent teenager who is a little shy. Most people think of him as a nerd until they get to know him. He is constantly involved in experiments and is always up for an academic challenge.

POWER LANCE™

Triceratops Dinozord™

The Triceratops Dinozord is extremely powerful and is armed with various weapons. It can move very fast and spear its enemy using its horns. Triceratops Dinozord is also capable of using chains and missiles to immobilize an enemy.

Though surrounded by enemies, the Blue Ranger's high-kicks will knock out enemies within seconds.

The Green Ranger has the strength of several human beings.

The Dragonzord lives in the ocean and responds to the musical call of the Dragonzord to help the Green Ranger. Using his powerful tail as a weapon, he can wipe out a whole horde of evil space aliens.

Dragonzord™

DRAGONSWORD™

TOMMY●GREEN RANGER
Tommy is the latest addition to the Power Rangers. He is also a martial arts expert and is very cool and calm. Though originally tricked by an evil spell into fighting the Power Rangers, he awakens and joins forces with the Power Rangers.

GREEN RANGER™

Tommy is the Green Ranger. Like the Red Ranger™, his martial arts training makes him a great fighter. His power comes from that of a Dragon. His weapon is the Dragon sword and his vehicle is the Dragonzord.

MIGHTY MORPHIN POWER RANGERS™

Protectors of Earth, the Power Rangers!! When the six Rangers come together as one, no enemy can stand in their way!! GO GO POWER RANGERS!